Go to www.av2books.com, and enter this book's unique code.

BOOK CODE

AVP65875

AV² by Weigl brings you media enhanced books that support active learning.

AV² provides enriched content that supplements and complements this book. Weigl's AV² books strive to create inspired learning and engage young minds in a total learning experience.

Your AV² Media Enhanced books come alive with...

 **Audio**
Listen to sections of the book read aloud.

 **Video**
Watch informative video clips.

 **Embedded Weblinks**
Gain additional information for research.

Try This!
Complete activities and hands-on experiments.

 **Key Words**
Study vocabulary, and complete a matching word activity.

 **Quizzes**
Test your knowledge.

 **Slide Show**
View images and captions, and prepare a presentation.

... and much, much more!

Published by AV² by Weigl
350 5th Avenue, 59th Floor New York, NY 10118
Website: www.av2books.com

Copyright ©2019 AV² by Weigl
All rights reserved. No part of this publication may be reproduced, stored in a retrieval system, or transmitted in any form or by any means, electronic, mechanical, photocopying, recording, or otherwise, without the prior written permission of Weigl Publishers Inc.

Library of Congress Control Number: 2018936771

ISBN 978-1-4896-7621-4 (hardcover)
ISBN 978-1-4896-7622-1 (softcover)
ISBN 978-1-4896-7623-8 (multi-user eBook)

Printed in the United States of America in Brainerd, Minnesota
1 2 3 4 5 6 7 8 9 0   22 21 20 19 18

032018
102517

Project Coordinator: John Willis
Art Director: Ana María Vidal

Every reasonable effort has been made to trace ownership and to obtain permission to reprint copyright material. The publisher would be pleased to have any errors or omissions brought to its attention so that they may be corrected in subsequent printings.

The publisher acknowledges Alamy, Dreamstime, Getty Images, iStock, and Shutterstock as the primary image suppliers for this title.

PARAMEDICS

CONTENTS

- 2 AV² Book Code
- 4 People who Keep Us Safe
- 6 Where a Paramedic Works
- 8 What is a Paramedic?
- 10 On the Way to the Hospital
- 12 Paramedic Tools
- 14 Cuts and Breaks
- 16 Breathing
- 18 Other Duties
- 20 Paramedics are Important
- 22 Paramedic Quiz
- 24 Key Words/Log on to www.av2books.com

Some people have jobs that help others stay safe.

The paramedic works to keep people safe.

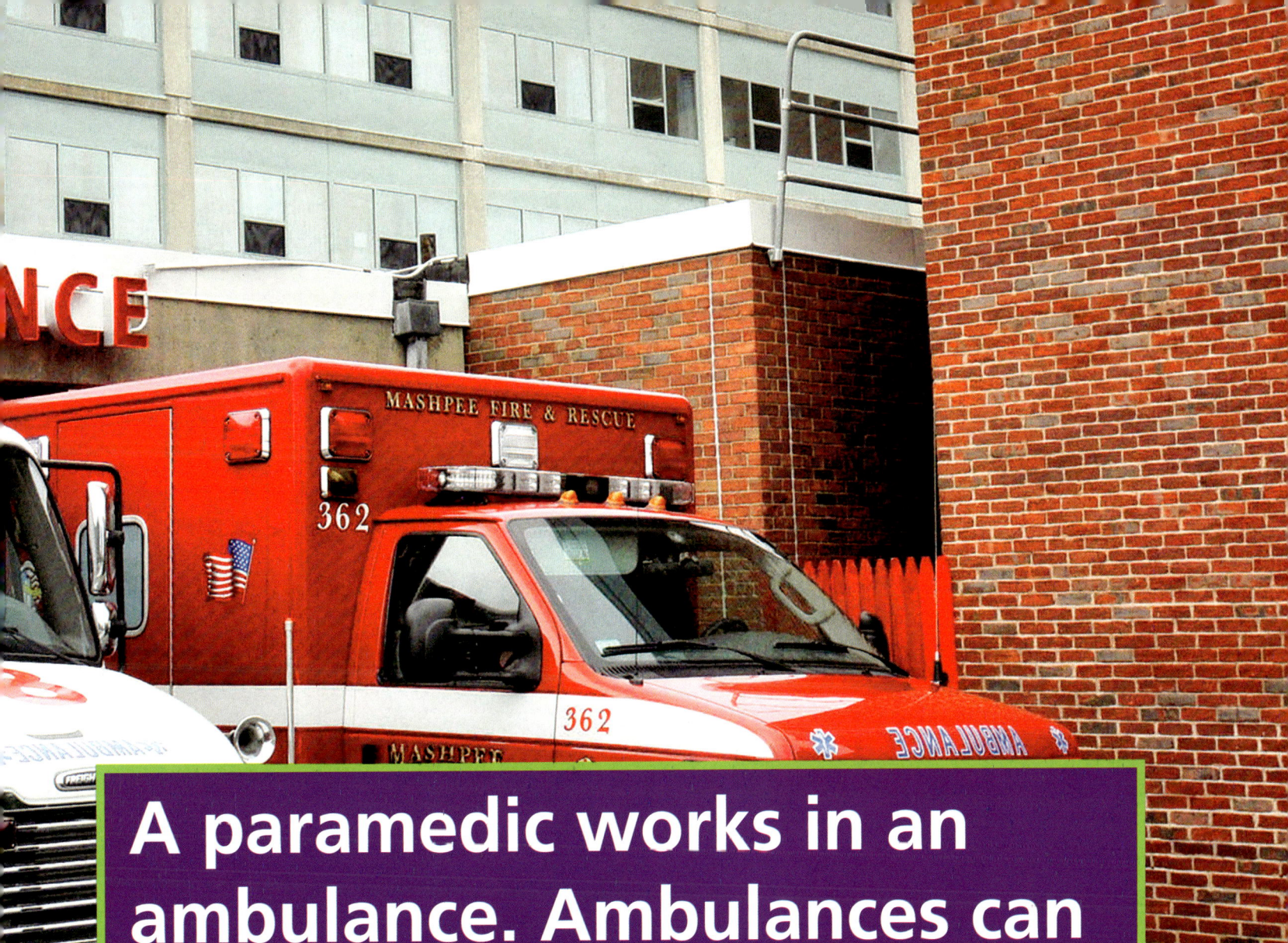

A paramedic works in an ambulance. Ambulances can take people who are badly hurt or very sick to hospitals.

A paramedic takes care of people before they get to the hospital.

He uses tools inside the ambulance to help them feel better.

9

The paramedic checks to see where someone is hurt.

10

He records what is wrong so he can tell the doctor.

The paramedic uses a special bed to move people from one place to another.

It has legs that fold up. This helps it fit inside an ambulance or helicopter.

The paramedic puts a bandage over cuts to keep them clean.

He uses a splint if a leg is broken. The splint keeps the leg still.

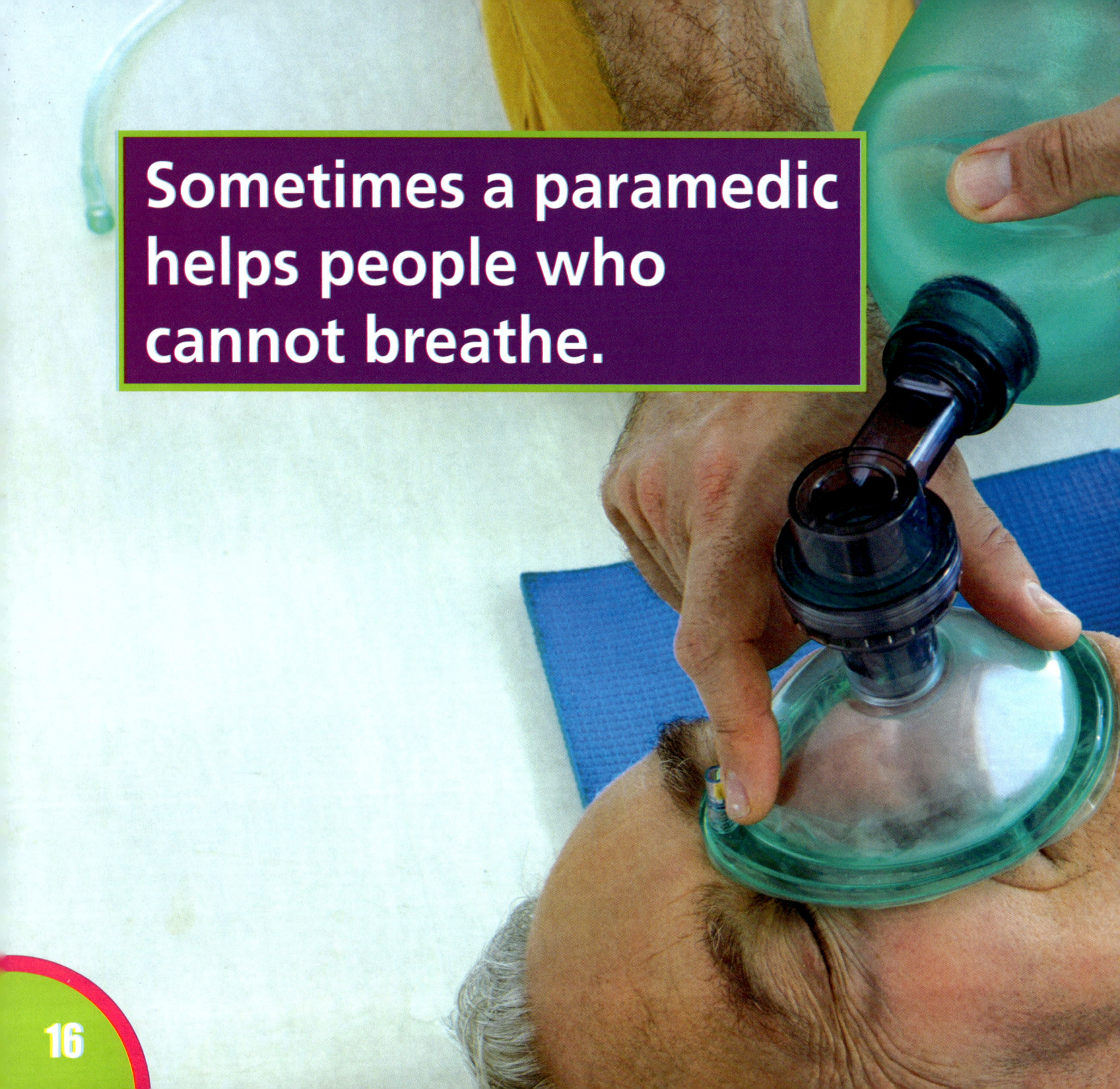

Sometimes a paramedic helps people who cannot breathe.

He uses a special machine to help them breathe again.

A paramedic must keep his ambulance clean at all times.

He also makes sure there are enough supplies for each day.

Paramedics are important because they keep us safe.

See what you have learned about paramedics.

KEY WORDS

Research has shown that as much as 65 percent of all written material published in English is made up of 300 words. These 300 words cannot be taught using pictures or learned by sounding them out. They must be recognized by sight. This book contains 63 common sight words to help young readers improve their reading fluency and comprehension. This book also teaches young readers several important content words, such as proper nouns. These words are paired with pictures to aid in learning and improve understanding.

Page	Sight Words First Appearance
4	have, help, others, people, some, that
5	keep, the, to, works
7	a, an, are, can, in, or, take, very, who
8	before, get, of, they
9	he, them, uses
10	is, see, where
11	so, tell, what
12	another, from, move, one, place
13	has, it, this, up
14	cuts, over, puts
15	if, still
16	sometimes
17	again
18	all, at, his, must, times
19	also, day, each, enough, for, makes, there
21	because, important, us

Page	Content Words First Appearance
4	jobs
5	paramedic
7	ambulance, hospitals
9	tools
11	doctor
12	bed
13	helicopter, legs
14	bandage
15	splint
17	machine
19	supplies

Check out www.av2books.com for activities, videos, audio clips, and more!

 Go to www.av2books.com.

 Enter book code.   AVP65875

 Fuel your imagination online!

www.av2books.com